# *Breathe in Grace*

### *A Zev Evans Novella*

# *James LePore*

DEDICATION:

## To my friend Peter Dalton.

The Story Plant
Studio Digital CT, LLC
PO Box 4331
Stamford, CT 06907

Story Plant Paperback ISBN-13: 978-1-61188-238-4
Fiction Studio Books E-book ISBN-13: 978-1-943486-92-2

Visit our website at www.thestoryplant.com
Visit the author's website at www.jamesleporefiction.com

First Story Plant Paperback Printing: June 2016

Printed in the United States of America

# CHAPTER 1

I took a break from the recital and went to a small alcove near the Pound Ridge Community Center's library. I would have smoked if I was still smoking but there is no smoking allowed anywhere in the world. Next to global warming, the worst thing that exists in the world is smoking. Third would be guns. I breathed deeply, something I do to replace cigarettes and to tamp down the constant low-grade anxiety I've lived with since I was a kid. I do mantras: *breathe in grace/breathe out anger,*

*breathe in pride/breathe out shame, breathe in clarity /breathe out confusion. . . . . . .*Sometimes the anxiety is high-grade. Then I have to take drastic measures, like a ten-mile run, or a weekend of good bourbon, or bad bourbon, it doesn't matter.

It's this anxiousness that got me thrown off the NYPD. (It also got me ejected from the Army, the end result of an incident I was involved in in Samarra in 2004. I will get to that later). Don't panic, I didn't kill anybody. I broke a guy's jaw and both arms one night when I was moonlighting as a half-assed security guard. I was twenty-two, a rookie, and was restless and pretty wound up after the intensity of the academy. I couldn't sleep much anyway, so when a friend of mine asked me if I wanted to make a hundred bucks watching some freight cars at the Fresh Pond Yard on Long Island, I gladly said yes. I asked my friend Johnny Scoglio, a fellow rookie, if he wanted to split the hundred with me. I knew he needed the money. He already had twin boys, and his wife was pregnant again. I heard a grunt and when I looked under one of the cars I saw Johnny flat on the ground and a guy all in black, including a black woolen hat, kneeling over him, pummeling him with a rock the size of a softball. I scrambled under the car and in under five seconds the guy was moaning on the ground. I lifted Johnny up and checked him out. There was a bruise on his temple and his left hand was hanging limp. I told him to go home, which he did.

It turns out the cars we were guarding were filled with fancy computers, and the guy on the ground was the yard foreman's son. The father went berserk, which to me was just a cover-up of his own criminal activity. You could only guess what it was. Likely getting the kid to cop a couple of laptops not knowing there would be two guys guarding the cars, not one. But the father had connections, so I was forced to resign. This was easy for the department to do as I was still in my probationary period, had few rights, and no friends higher up. The kid smirked the whole time at the review board hearing. His jaw had been unwired at that point, but it was satisfying to see that his arms were still in casts. Also, I think the smirking might have been painful, so that was a good thing too. There's always a silver lining.

Of course you're noticing how I digress. It's the anxiety. To return to the subject, when I was in the alcove doing my breathing exercises, I heard a man and a woman arguing. I looked around the corner and saw them a short distance away, at the end of the hall near a wall-to-ceiling window. I stepped out of the alcove to let them know I was nearby, but they didn't notice. I liked the alcove and am not one to cede territory, so I just stood there, hoping that when they spotted me they'd go someplace else to argue. I could now hear them better than when I was in the alcove.

"You're done when I say you're done," the guy said.

"I can't do it," she said. "I can't."

The guy grabbed her arm and she tried to pull away, but he pulled her back to him. They were standing close to each other now, face to face. If you had just come on this scene you would think they were lovers about to kiss passionately. Rhett Butler and Scarlett O'Hara. Instead of kissing her, he held her tightly by the shoulder with his left hand and slapped her across the face with his right. *Whack.* Her head jerked to the side.

She tried to pull away again, but he pulled her back and said something I couldn't hear, a smile on his face that that really wasn't a smile.

He spotted me then. We took a good look at each other. He had dark eyes and a beard with a white line in it—a scar where the hair didn't grow. I usually don't like people looking at me, but in these situations, the reverse is true. I wanted him to really see me, to remember me. He let go of the woman's arm and gave her a slight nudge. She slipped past him and walked away.

I never saw her face—her back was to me the whole time—but I made a quick assessment as she made her way to the exit at the end of the hallway. Tall, maybe five-eight, short brown hair and a good shape, by that I mean some meat on her bones. She held her head high. *Good for you*, I thought. *Fuck him.* The silver buckles on her boots sparkled for a second as she stepped into the bright sunlight. When I turned back, the guy was gone.

I decided to head home. I go to the community center to listen to live music. It's one of the few things that calms me, that lulls the wild horses that stampede in my head when they're not grazing or sleeping, which is not often. This one was Christmas songs by a gal playing piano all alone on the stage, very jazzy, very pretty. But the guy with the scar had ruined it. I am a worrier and now I was worried about the woman with the nice body and the silver buckles on her boots, and what would happen if she didn't do what the guy with the scar wanted her to do.

# CHAPTER 2

When I start worrying, I have to do something. Otherwise . . . well, otherwise things will not be good for me, or for the people around me, which is why I live alone. I do not go off half-cocked, however. I can act deliberately when there is no immediate danger. Even when there is, I am pretty cool. In this case, I was lucky. I saw scarface walking to his car, followed him, and memorized his license plate. If I hadn't done that I would have lost a week of my life worrying and probably drinking way too much.

Fortunately for my liver and my mental state, Johnny Scoglio, who now has four kids and a master's in computer science, is the head of computer security at the NYPD's Counterterrorism Bureau. To get this job you basically have to be the world's best hacker, which Johnny probably is, although this is something known to no one except me and the chief of his bureau. Johnny thinks he owes me because I lost my job that night at Fresh Pond and he didn't. He doesn't, but if he did, he's paid me back a hundred times over. He has gotten me information that has saved my life more than once. He also has many friends throughout the counterterrorism law enforcement world in the U.S. and overseas. He doesn't care about search warrants and probable cause. He has fed information, all of it illegally obtained, to colleagues at local, state, federal, and international agencies, that has prevented more than one mass killing. He is a god in their minds. His bureau chief, a crusty Jew who fought in the Israeli army before migrating to New York, allows Johnny to do this because he knows that in a crisis, if he ever needs a favor in a hurry, he can call on about a hundred people who will drop everything to help him, which of course means helping the people of New York, the greatest city there is.

Scarface's plate came back to Mohammed Asani, age forty, at an address in the Bronx. Mohammed immigrated from Tunisia in 2007 and got permanent status when he married an American woman, Linda Manning, in that same year. The picture Johnny sent me of Manning was of a woman with medium length blonde hair and blue eyes. Was it the woman Asani slapped? Maybe. I had only seen her from behind. She could have cut and dyed her hair. Asani was naturalized in 2010. His picture matched the guy I saw at the concert, the slapper, including the beard and the scar on his right cheek. At the bottom, Johnny wrote, *No known TT's*, his shorthand for terrorist ties. So Mohammed was just another new American citizen toiling away at whatever in the most densely insane of New York's five boroughs. And slapping women in the face during a piano recital in rural Westchester County.

I would pay Mohammed a visit. I couldn't get him bracing her with his left hand and hitting her with his right out of my head, of her head snapping sideways. I needed to replace it. What would I do when I met up with him? I don't know. I'm a jumble of nerve endings. I sometimes let them dictate events.

Before I saw Asani, I would stop by and see my friend Eva, who lived not too far from him in the Bronx. Eva is a hot Cuban woman who calls me Popi and sometimes will have sex with me, though not lately as her husband is visiting from Mexico. She sends me clients and had called to say one was ready to retain me. She had 5K in cash for me. I do not kill people, except in self-defense, but I will do quite a bit in service to a paying client. I should have said this earlier, but I don't think now is too late: I am a fixer. If you have a problem that the police can't help you with, or that you do not have the skill set or nerve to handle yourself, I am your man. The five thousand I was picking up from Eva was the first installment on a fee of 10K. I don't start work until I get the full fee. I give Eva a ten percent referral fee. Also, sometimes she works with me on a case and I'll pay her. Sometimes if she needs me to do something for her I'll help her out for free. That's when the sex is best, as she likes to refer to herself at certain crescendo moments as Popi's little *puta*. She almost drowned coming over on a raft from Castro's worker's paradise when she was fourteen and has since helped many others escape. As a result, she is owed many favors and has developed a set of balls bigger than most guys I know. I don't know why she married the Mexican, a fat little asshole, but that's not my business.

# CHAPTER 3

Eva lives in East Tremont, which is, I feel safe in say-ing, one of the worst neighborhoods in the country. It's all five and six story tenements, no trees, garbage in the streets, with gangbangers, drugs, and fear everywhere. The last time I was at her apartment there were two black kids taking turns whacking an ATM machine with a sledgehammer on the sidewalk in front of her build-ing. This was in broad daylight. People passed them like it was nothing, which is the best strategy to have if you live there. Don't notice, or, if you do, look away quickly, or better yet, cross the street. Fast. Everything is nothing until it happens to you. When it does happen to you, you could easily be maimed or dead. Being able to, one, not notice, and two, run, are very important survival skills in the ghetto. If I was a television network I'd do a reality series where they drop a suburban couple in the ghetto and follow them as they try to survive. That's just one of the many oddball things that occur to me as I breeze through my days and nights. If you continue reading, you will probably hear more of them so please bear with me. It's a tic that I have given up fighting.

If you're wondering how Eva can live here and not get raped or killed, it's because the first two floors of her building are taken up by a guy named Edison (I don't know his last name, and wouldn't tell you if I did) and his large family. Edison is the head of a Jamaican gang that has taken over most of the rackets in Tremont. Eva calls him *el jefe*. They have done business together for years and no one will cross her or disturb her in any way lest Edison does something unspeakable to them. I have met Edison in passing a couple of times and I think he knows that I too am capable of doing unspeakable things, so I am allowed to come and go.

Eva keeps mannequins in her apartment. She says she has plans of making clothes and selling them, but I've never seen one of her mannequins with clothes on. They're always naked. Some have limbs missing, or the limbs stick out at weird angles. On some, she's used a magic marker to rearrange their faces. What Eva does best, the only thing she does as far as I can see, is broker things. She won't get you an untraceable gun, but she'll connect you to someone who can. You want to move some stolen jewelry, she'll hook you up. You need some forged documents, she'll send you to the right person. Etcetera. For these connections, she takes a fee. This means that people have to trust her, on both sides of the transaction, which is an amazing thing in the ghetto, but she's pulled it off.

The client that Eva has currently hooked me up with is an old guy named Jose whose grandson needs a kidney transplant. They're both illegal. The kid's fourteen years old and in end-stage renal failure. He gets his dialysis three times a week at the ER, which New York pays for. The kid's parents are dead. The grandfather is too old and is not a match anyway. The waiting list is a hundred thousand-plus, which the kid can get on, but, assuming by some miracle he gets near the top quickly, will have to prove he can pay for post-op care, which is expensive. ("*No way, Jose,*" said Eva, making a dumb joke). They want to go back to Guatemala for the surgery. They have been in contact with a broker, who says fifteen thousand dollars will cover everything. They want me to travel with them to protect them and the cash they'll be carrying and to make sure they don't get fucked. I have done some research on transplant tourism, and am skeptical of a lot of things relating to the deal. Nevertheless, because it's Eva, I've agreed to talk to the grandfather.

"You're early," she says.

"I thought we'd catch up."

"You mean fuck."

"Is that so bad?" I tried to look sheepish and thought I pulled it off. Of course, I'm no judge.

"Hector's here."

"Where?"

"Sleeping."

13

"I can give him a sedative."

"Popi . . ."

"I have to make another stop," I say. "I'll be back."

"Where?"

"Bronx River Avenue, near the Expressway."

"For what?"

"Business."

"How long will it take?"

"An hour. I'm not sure."

"OK, Jose is coming at nine."

"Maybe you can help me," I said. "I'm looking for a guy named Asani. He's got a beard with a white scar line."

I watched the look in Eva's big brown eyes change from playful to serious.

"You know him?" I asked.

"No."

"What?"

"There's a mosque over there in a strip mall. I hear the head guy has a beard with a scar line."

She had my full attention. Not that she didn't before, but this was a different kind of attention. "Yes," I said, "*and?*"

"That's just it. There's no and."

"Nothing?"

"No, and you know this neighborhood. There are no secrets here. Everybody's up everybody else's ass. I would have heard *something*."

I smiled.

"Why are you smiling?" Eva asked. "I'm being serious."

"I like when you say ass."

"Popi."

"Say it again."

"Ass."

"Say pussy."

"Pussy."

"How about that sedative?" I said. I reached into my jacket pocket, where I keep a small pharmacopeia in a leather pouch. My anti-seizure pills, Phenobarbital, which I haven't taken in eleven years but keep renewing the prescription, are in it, along with a couple of throwaway syringes in cellophane and vials of various things that are useful to have on hand in case they're needed.

"Popi . . ."

"Yes, *mi amado*."

"That look in your eyes."

"Yes?"

"It is like a drug to me."

"Good."

"But Hector goes back to Mexico tonight. He'll miss his flight. You don't want that."

"Right. I'll see you later."

# CHAPTER 4

The address I had been given for Asani was in a small strip mall set below street level. Looming behind it was one of the brick and concrete walls that carried the Cross Bronx Expressway over and through what I have been told was once the leafiest of New York's five boroughs, but was now a shithole of crime and anger. I parked in the parking lot of a bar next door and climbed over a rusted-out cyclone fence to the so-called mall, which consisted of four stores with glass doors and plate glass windows. No lights were on in any unit. Diagonal parking bays, all empty, ran across the front with a sidewalk in between. Next to the mosque was a tax preparer's office. The units on either end were dark and looked untenanted. I can smell alarm systems, and the mosque's front door definitely looked wired. Arabic lettering on the plate glass window read: East Tremont Islamic Center. I know this because I read and speak Arabic (and a couple of other languages). The guttural sounds of the Middle East come easy to me, probably because I am half Jew. The other half is Sicilian. My life story is interesting, but not really relevant now. My name—another oversight, sorry—is Zev Evans. My friends, the few that I have, call me Z, or Zevon (a reference to the half-moon scar on the top of my head where an Army doctor put a plate in to patch a hole in my skull in 2004. Like Levon from the Elton John song, I wear my war wound like a crown. It's their idea of a joke).

I went around back where a narrow alley butted up against the twenty-foot high concrete Expressway wall. Cars and trucks whizzed by above. Two cars were parked in the alley, a black SUV and a small red Toyota. The mosque's back door was impregnable—reinforced steel, with a heavy-duty lockset, probably also wired. The tax place next door had the same reinforced steel back door with the same lockset. There was a small rear window for each unit that had been bricked up. On the roof, I saw nothing that would get me in, so I gave up. As I was about to climb down, two people came out of the back door of the tax place, a woman in a hijab and Mohammed Asani. The woman was carrying a small white box. The woman got into the Toyota and Asani got into the SUV.

I am not a big guy, six-one, one-eighty, and still young at thirty-eight. The point, not well made, I admit, is I can be cat-like. I can stalk someone and then approach them from behind and they would never know anything was amiss until they were dead or rendered helpless. I was thrown out of the Army because I stalked and killed the allegedly wrong guy one night outside Samarra. There was a big uproar because the guy was supposedly on our side. I didn't think he was, and the Army must have had its doubts because there was no court martial. Instead, I was quietly, and honorably, discharged. And forcibly, too, as I wanted to try to stay in, but was told I had no choice

Another digression, sorry.

I waited until the two cars left the alley and then slipped down. In about fifteen seconds I was in my truck, an armored Land Cruiser, facing Bronx River Avenue. I had seen both Asani and the hijab woman turn left. At the next corner, Asani turned left and the woman right. I followed the woman. (I knew where to find Asani). An hour later, most of it on The Long Island Expressway heading east, she pulled off of Route 27, a two-lane highway, onto a dirt road that went through some woods and ended at a chain-link fence. My head-lights off, I backed into a small cutout in the trees about a hundred feet away and watched. A few minutes later runway lights went on and a small plane landed and taxied to a stop in a field on the other side of the fence. A man got out, walked to the fence, reached over, and took the small white box from the hijab woman.

# CHAPTER 5

As I was driving back to her place, I called Eva to apologize for being late. It was getting on to 9 p.m. She said that her husband was drunk and would miss his flight, that she had called Jose and that I should visit him at his apartment in Queens. She gave me his address. Jose's building was a block from the Whitestone Bridge, which did not portend well, as, in my experience, major city bridges spread grime and blight twenty blocks in all directions. As I approached his street, I saw two prostitutes on the corner. One was leggy, in a red leather jacket and a skirt so short it might not have been there. Maybe it wasn't. The other was chunky with a big, blonde wig. I felt bad for them because it was so cold, but they seemed relaxed as they chatted, steam coming out of their mouths. I looked around for their pimp and there he was, in an Escalade at the curb opposite them, the motor running, keeping warm, talking on his cell phone. I was sure he had a gun, the newest Glock. I would, that's for sure, if I were sitting in a fifty thousand dollar car, running whores near the Whitestone Bridge in Queens. All three watched me with interest as I turned onto Jose's street. The block surprised me. It was crappy, but it was redeemed by pride. Garbage cans were lined up neatly in front of two- and three-family houses that were sagging and worn out but that were obviously home to people who had gotten close to the bottom but were not yet giving up. Mixed in were a couple of old-fashioned brick apartment buildings and even a few side-by-side one-families. A couple of these had smoke coming from chimneys; I could smell the firewood burning. When I got home that's the first thing I'd do, light a fire and sip a cognac in front of it before attempting to sleep, always a fifty-fifty proposition with me.

Jose's apartment was in the basement of one of the apartment buildings. He undid some locks and greeted me graciously. His hair white as snow, he was dressed in a red cardigan sweater and old work pants.

"It's a Christmas gift from my grandson," he said.

I guess I had been staring at the sweater. I accepted his offer of a beer as I felt it would be disrespectful to say no or ask for anything else. I like beer, so that helped. The grandson, Miguel, in his pajamas, was sitting at the kitchen table, writing in a notebook. At his feet, looking at me with his eyes half closed, was what looked like a mix of German Shepherd and about five other breeds of dog.

"Homework," Jose said.

"Senor," Miguel said, when we were introduced. The kid did not look good. He was a sickly pale yellow, and rail thin—I could see the outline of his rib cage under his pajama top—with dark gray circles under his sunken eyes. At fourteen.

We sat in a small parlor, me on a couch with a multi-colored wool blanket draped over it, and Jose on a wooden rocker facing me. A white plastic Christmas tree stood in a corner. It was decorated with small red lights in the shape of apples that blinked intermittently as we talked.

"Did you get your money?" Jose asked.

"I didn't take it."

"Why not?"

"You're going to the worst place in the world for a transplant."

"I have relatives there. Miguel can heal with them."

"Fifteen thousand dollars is really cheap."

"Thank God."

"Too cheap."

Jose was silent for a beat. Then he said, "that's all I have, plus your fee."

"How did you raise all this cash?"

"The neighborhood."

"The neighborhood?"

"Donations in jars. Also I have saved for the past ten years. Nickels, dimes, dollars."

"Saved for what?"

"For Miguel. He was born with bad kidneys. *Malos rinones. Dos.*"

The old man handed me a brochure titled ARPKD. I stuck it in my pocket.

"What do you do?" I asked.

"I am a janitor. I clean the Chinese dance hall on Linden Place. I take care of this building. Other buildings. I can fix things. They call me sometimes in the middle of the night."

"How old are you, Jose?"

"Fifty-five."

He looked seventy-five.

"Do you know what sepsis is?"

"Yes."

"Rejection?"

"Yes."

"How are you going to pay for the anti-rejection drugs? They'll probably cost another ten thousand, maybe more."

"I will find a way."

"Do you know where they get their kidneys?"

"No."

"Have you seen the facility? Is it a hospital?"

"No. I don't know."

"Who gets the fifteen thousand dollars?"

"A man here in Queens gets two thousand five hundred. The rest I give to the doctor."

"Directly to the doctor?"

"No, to another man in Guate."

"Guate?"

"Guatemala City."

I nodded, then said: "people get ripped off."

"That's why I need you."

"I was told that to get it done right, you need a hundred thousand dollars. And definitely not to go to Guatemala."

"I don't have that kind of money."

"Who's the man who gets the twenty-five hundred dollars?"

"He's a lawyer."

"A lawyer?"

"Abogado."

*Abogado*, I knew, covered a lot of bases in the low-end Hispanic community. A lot of bases.

"I have to talk to him before I give you an answer."

"No."

"No?"

"He will walk away."

"Jose . . ." I was about to walk away myself, but before I could say anything, the dog came over and sat next to me. We looked at each other for a second or two.

"Donato," said Jose.

"Donato?"

"The dog. He likes you. His name means Gift from God."

I could see out of the corner of my eye that Donato was still staring at me.

"May I ask you a question, senor Zev?"

"Yes, of course."

"Do you have *convulsiones*?"

I took a breath. I had had one seizure in my life.

"*Lo siento,*" said Jose.

I shook my head.

"Donato," said Jose, "was given to us by a friend who had to go back to Guatemala. He . . ."

"Yes, Jose, he what?"

"He knows *epilepticos.*"

I nodded.

"If a seizure is coming," said Jose, "he knows. He can stop it."

I shook my head again, in denial that we were talking about this.

"My friend's son was *epilectico,*" said Jose. "He died last week and my friend took him back to Guatemala to be buried with his mother and two sisters."

I said nothing. I could feel my gut tightening. The dog was still looking at me.

"You saw Miguel," Jose said.

Again I was silent.

"He will be dead in six months. He is my only grandchild."

*Good*, I said to myself, the subject has been changed. "How did he get here?" I asked.

"On a bus last summer. I met him at the *hielo* in Texas."

He meant an ICE facility at the border.

"I have to go."

"Si, senor."

"Don't pay the lawyer yet," I said. "I'll get back to you."

# CHAPTER 6

While I was sipping my cognac, I got a fax from Johnny Scoglio, who I had called on the drive to Queens from Long Island. It was the registration for the hijab lady's car. Its owner was Rashida Nahra, with an address in Queens. Another fax followed, a homicide investigation report signed by NYPD Homicide Detective Joseph P. Seritella. Linda Asani, nee Manning, had killed herself with a huge dose of Ambien. Under the heading *Pre-ter-minal Circumstances* was the summary of a statement from the deceased's husband, M. Asani: *Deceased was very depressed. She could not sleep. She took Ambien to sleep, and Paxil for depression. She must have been hoarding the Ambien. She had had several surgeries prior to their marriage that she would not talk about. Husband says possibly cancer, possibly woman's problems, but husband doesn't know.*

*Husband is an "imam." Deceased was born in California and met husband on a church trip to Jordan. Deceased has no relatives. They are all deceased. She is an only child. She was extremely depressed lately. Her psychiatrist is Dr. Ahmed Abdul-Samad, Mount Vernon. Dr. Abdul confirmed insomnia and severe depression. His px records were in order.*

Across the top Johnny had written, *what's up?*

I had the same question. It was close to midnight. I felt like I could sleep, but have had bad experiences with this feeling. It is not reliable. I brought my laptop to bed and went online. There was no Dr. Ahmed Abdul-Samad in Mount Vernon or anywhere else in New York. I looked in all fifty states. Nothing. I looked at the clock display on my cable box. I had been tempted to try Ambien myself, but resisted. If I could get a few hours every night, or even every other night, I functioned pretty good. Abdul-Samad might be dead, or had his license revoked, or retired, or changed careers.

On the New York State Department of Health's website, I found this:

> Name: Ahmed Abdul-Samad
> Address: Yonkers, NY
> Profession: Medicine
> License No: 2808577
> Date of Licensure: 07/03/09
> Additional Qualification: n/a
> Status: Voluntarily surrendered.
> Registered through last day of: 06/11
> Medical School: University of Jordan
> Degree Date: 05/27/2001

I looked at the time again. It was now officially Christmas Eve 2015. I thought about Jose and Miguel, about Jose's red sweater and Miguel's sunken eyes. That plastic Christmas tree with those blinking apples. Jose had wished me a Merry Christmas as I was leaving. I couldn't take his money, but I couldn't let them go to Guatemala by themselves. They would be robbed and killed in the first six hours they were there. I thought about the three women who had come into my life at the winter solstice. One getting slapped in the face at a Christmas concert, her head snapping sideways, one getting into a car on a freezing winter night and driving out to a small airport on Long Island, and one dead.

Who were they and why did I give a shit about them?

# CHAPTER 7

On Christmas Eve day I sat by the fire and sipped Jack Daniels. I put a nine-hour loop on my computer called Tibetan Healing Sounds. Water gurgling, birds chirping, bells, crickets, all this muted stuff. Music notes mixed in with dust motes and drifted around my two-room cottage all day. Notes and motes. I had spent many Christmases and Christmas Eves since 2004 among them. For food, I made rice and beans and ate it three times. I put a big bowl out for Moishe Dayan, the cockeyed little feral black cat who lived somewhere behind my house. Every so often I went outside to look at the sky, which was silent and thick with unmoving bloated gray clouds all day. When I went out at six, the clouds had gotten wispy and a full moon was rising behind some trees. I wished it a Merry Christmas. I thought about my three women, about young Miguel, and about the dog, Donato.

I had had my one seizure after my brain injury in 2004, while I was still in the hospital. You have epilepsy if you have more than one seizure. Since I've never had another one, I don't have epilepsy, or you could say I don't have it yet. I've heard of seizure alert dogs and seizure assist dogs, but the docs who have studied the issue say it's bullshit. They say it in a nice way, but that's what it comes down to. Plus when I was eleven I watched as my first and only dog, a mutt I found in a vacant lot, got run over by a truck. That must have gone deep as I've never even thought of having a dog since.

At seven o'clock I went to a church service at the community center. When I got back, there was a fax on my computer from Johnny Scoglio: Linda Manning's autopsy report. The Ambien—zolpidem tartrate—was confirmed in liver and stomach specimens. I went to church on Christmas and Easter out of respect for my mother. I was a handful, often uncontrollable. She was the Sicilian. She used to take me to church, St. Rocco's in Glen Cove, and pray for me. I used to ask her where the soul was in the body. She'd say everywhere, every cell. What's a cell? The tiniest piece of every thing in your body, she answered. Looking at the pictures of Linda's specimen slides reminded me of those conversations. Was I looking at her soul, this woman who had met an "imam" in Jordan, married him and killed herself four years later? On her autopsy pictures there were fresh scars where the liver had been accessed and the stomach removed. There was also an old scar extending diagonally eight inches up from her belly button and under her rib cage.

# CHAPTER 8

The guy I killed in Samarra was a very bad guy. He was, however, working for us, which I did not know at the time I killed him. He was standing outside our perimeter one night whispering on his phone. We had set up camp near the main bridge across the Tigris, which we had secured that day. While we were securing the bridge, speedboats, which we saw were piled with weapons, began racing across the river. They were destroyed, about twenty in all, by M1 and howitzer fire. On guard duty, which I loved, because, as you know, I couldn't sleep, I thought I heard a strange noise on the river bank. Exploring, I came upon a rowboat in some bulrushes, and then the guy on the phone. I put my M9 into the small of his back before he knew I was there. Unfortunately for me, and for him, he dropped and whipped his legs at me, a pretty professional move. He also pulled a weapon, another M9. Before he could swing it toward me I shot him dead, taking the top of his head off. I then heard the unmistakable whine of incoming mortar fire and hit the ground.

The next thing I knew, I was in a hospital bed in Landstulh, Germany, looking at a woman sitting next to me holding my hand. This woman turned out to be Carol Harris, the Army doc who aspirated my swollen brain cavity, put my plate in, and prescribed my seizure meds, the ones I don't take, but keep renewing, don't ask me why. She basically saved my life, as I was told that things got pretty dicey in my brain in the eighteen hours it took to get me from Samarra to Baghdad to Landstuhl. I returned the favor three years later, but that story can wait for another day. The thing is, we're still friends.

I believe the guy I killed was giving some other bad guys the coordinates of our base camp. He must have gotten them wrong, or his hajji friends did, because our camp was a quarter mile away. As I said before, the brass must have had their doubts about him, because they were not hard on me, even though the guy's family and friends put up a huge stink. Self-righteous bullshit like, *is this how our friendship is repaid?* They wanted compensation and they probably got it. The Army must have been happy I got that injury. I was already known as a troublemaker, and they had a perfect excuse to get rid of me and placate the guy's backers. I readily admitted, by the way, that I had shot the guy, and told anyone who would listen that he was double-crossing us.

Over bourbon and cheese and crackers—my Christmas Eve dinner—I sent an e-mail to Carol Harris to ask her where the best places to get a kidney transplant were if you needed it in a hurry, and the cost. As an afterthought, I sent her Linda Asani's autopsy report and pictures. I was curious about the scar on her abdomen. Next, I looked up Rashida Nahra's address in Queens. The Google Earth picture showed a peeling one-family house on a dead-end street off of Queens Boulevard. The back yard abutted The Long Island Expressway. No car was in the narrow driveway. In the back yard, which was separated from the highway by a chain-link fence, was a detached one-car garage. Cars whizzed by on the highway.

At church, I prayed that I did not have another seizure. I know this is selfish, given all the suffering in the world, but I live alone and at Christmas I always think of death and dying. I should say here that no one knows my medical situation except Carol Harris and Johnny Scoglio. I never told my mother, who died in her sleep five years ago, because she would have gone crazy with novenas and rosaries and more covert Sicilian stuff. She didn't need that at her age. My dad, a Mossad agent by then, was already dead, killed in a car bombing in Beirut in 2005.

# CHAPTER 9

Early on the day after Christmas, I parked on Queens Boulevard and waited for Rashida Nahra to exit her street. We had had a white Christmas, but it wasn't too pretty in Queens on the day after. I brought lunch and a thermos of coffee, but didn't need them. Rashida came out in her red Toyota and turned right onto Queens Boulevard at eight a.m. I followed her to Northern Westchester Hospital in Mount Kisco, a ninety-minute drive that took us out of the grimy city into a different world (it might as well have been a different planet)—rural and wealthy Westchester County. At the hospital she entered an employee's parking garage. On my phone, I looked up RN's in New York and found that Rashida was one. She was also listed on the nursing staff at Northern Westchester as a Perioperative Nurse/First Assistant. I was about to leave when I saw Rashida walk out of the corner entrance of the garage with another woman. Both were in winter coats, boots and scarves. Rashida had on her hijab. I saw some flashes of light blue between the hems of their coats and the tops of their boots as they picked their way through ice and slush to the hospital next door. The second woman was taller than Rashida by a head. She had the hood of her coat up so I couldn't see much of her face or whether her hair was long or short, but her boots had silver buckles on them. I took their picture with my phone.

On the way home—only a few miles away—I called Johnny Scoglio and asked if he could set up a meeting with Joe Seritella.

# CHAPTER 10

"How are you, Z?" said Johnny.

"Pretty good. How are you?"

"OK." I could see that the knuckles on his left hand—he was sipping coffee from a chipped mug—were swollen and red.

"Johnny says you were in the academy together," said Seritella, who was sitting next to Johnny, across from me at a diner in Mount Vernon, which is the town you enter when you leave the Bronx at its north end. He had gripped my hand pretty hard when we were introduced. I looked at his hand when we disengaged. It was thick and calloused, a blunt instrument. A barrel-chested guy with a big gut, he looked more like a punched-out boxer than a detective.

I nodded. "Thanks for coming."

Seritella waited for me to say something else, but I didn't.

"So you want to know about the suicide with the hijab," he said.

"She was wearing a hijab?"

Seritella nodded.

"When?"

"At the hospital. The husband wouldn't let them take it off."

"Was she alive?"

"No. D.O.A."

"What hospital?"

"Mount Sinai."

"Is that where you took his statement?"

"There and back at his mosque. He was fighting an autopsy, saying it was against his religion, but he had no choice. I wanted to see the crime scene, so we went back there."

"Was it really a mosque?" I asked.

"Who knows? There were no chairs, and a pile of mats against a wall."

"When did he tell you about her prior surgeries?"

"*When*?"

"At the hospital or at the mosque?"

"It's not in my report?"

"No."

"I don't remember."

"Did he have a scar on his face?"

"Yes."

"Did you ask him about it?"

Seritella shook his head. "I don't remember. It's not in my report?"

"No."

"What are you working on?" Seritella asked.

"I'm just looking into something," I said.

He nodded, and said, "OK, what else?"

"Did you talk to the other tenants?"

"No."

"*Were* there other tenants?"

"There was a dry cleaner and a nail joint."

"There are four units."

"I don't remember the fourth."

"The husband."

"A scumbag."

"Was he really an imam?" I was thinking of those quotes around imam in Seritella's report, a grammatical touch that I appreciated even more, now that I'd met him. He was no Hemingway.

"I don't know, like I said, a scumbag."

"Your report says they were living in Mount Vernon."

"Yes."

"Where did she do it?"

"In the kitchen of the mosque, in the back. That's why we had jurisdiction. That's where the husband found her."

"Was there a window back there?"

"A window?"

"Yes."

"I don't remember."

"I'll tell you why I ask," I said. "I looked up the tax records for the strip mall. It's owned by Mohammed Asani. Assessed value: two hundred ninety thousand. He bought it in 2009 for two hundred thousand. No mortgage. I also looked up the permits when it was built in 1985. The plans have small windows at the back of each unit. There are none there now. They're bricked up."

"So what are you thinking?"

"Privacy, security."

"OK, I agree."

"The time of death matched up?"

"Yes."

The top-heavy detective screwed up his mouth. He was trying to be patient, I could tell, but not succeeding.

"Why was the husband a scumbag?" I asked.

"I got a call from community affairs."

"About what?"

"CAIR filed a complaint. They said I was harassing the guy because he was Muslim."

"Were you?"

"A little. He was breaking the nurse's balls at the hospital. She wanted to take the hijab off, to compose the body."

"What happened?"

"I had to give a statement, all that bullshit."

"What kind of bullshit?"

"Diversity training."

"Really?"

"Bloomberg, de Blasio, it's all been downhill since Giuliani."

"Did it stick? Are you a good obedient cop now? You love all the people's of the world?"

"They forced me to retire."

"I didn't know that."

"CAIR wouldn't quit."

"What are you doing?"

"Investigation for an injury lawyer."

I said nothing.

"It helps," he said. "I got a grown son with autism."

"Will you do me a favor?"

"Are you going to kill this guy?"

"I don't know."

"What's the favor?"

"There's an airport out east. Levendusky. Private, no tower. Wikipedia says it's been closed since 2014."

"What about it?"

"Someone's using it at night. A single engine. I want to know who."

"OK."

"The runway lights should be disabled," I said, "it's an FAA rule when you close an airport. Someone's turning them on. Probably just a circuit breaker. I want to know who."

"No problem."

"I don't want it stopped. I just want to know who's doing this."

Seritella nodded. "Anything else?"

"You feel like watching the husband?"

"Happily."

"There's no money."

"I've heard about you."

I nodded. I wasn't surprised.

"Maybe you'll do me a favor some day."

"That's how the world works, Joe."

…

Johnny and I watched Seritella get into his Buick through the diner's plate glass window.

"He's motivated," I said, watching him drive off.

Johnny nodded. "We got lucky," he said.

"How did you get him to agree to meet me?"

"He called a couple of people. They vouched for me."

"You're a legend."

"Thanks to you."

"For getting your wrist crushed and almost losing your job?"

Johnny had told his commanding officer that he had fallen at home while trying to fix a leaky shower. The CO, a good guy who had seen a lot of bullshit, a lot of good and bad cops, had put him on a desk and sent him to computer school.

"Danielle is forever grateful," Johnny said.

"How is she?"

"Good. She went back to work."

"At the lawyer's office?"

"Yes."

"The kids?"

"They're good."

"You?"

"Good."

I looked at him. He looked OK, except for the swelling in his left hand and the thick scarring on his wrist, where he had had his two surgeries.

"The hand?"

"It's OK."

"It doesn't look good."

"It's the cold, Z."

"When I'm finished with this guy, Asani, we'll go to the desert, hunt snakes."

"You know I don't hunt."

"You can watch."

Johnny Scoglio, a simple guy with a simple life and a genius IQ, smiled, which is what I wanted to see.

"You didn't tell me Seritella was retired," I said.

"I didn't know myself. I called him on his cell."

Johnny, I knew, could get anybody's cell number as long they had an account with a carrier, domestic or international. He could also access the numbers assigned to throwaway phones and listen in if he wanted to, a needle-in-a-haystack undertaking if there ever was one. He should be running the NSA's monitoring operations, which I've told him many times, but he's content to do his magic for the NYPD and go home at five o'clock to Danielle and the kids—the twins, now fully grown, and two girls that came later, with a miscarriage in between, that being the baby, another boy, in Danielle's belly when Johnny got banged up at Fresh Pond. I blame myself for that miscarriage and think about that lost baby a lot.

"What's going on?" Johnny asked.

"I need to talk to a nurse at Northern Westchester Hospital."

"You don't have a name?"

"No."

"A description?"

"Five-eight, white, thirty-something. Nice body. Short brown hair. I'll send you a picture."

"That shouldn't be too hard."

"And if you can get me Asani's financials."

"OK."

"Aren't you going to ask me why?"

"No."

I smiled, and so did Johnny. I'm not depressed or bitter, but I don't smile much. My mother used to call me Abraham Lincoln, her idea of the most serious man who ever lived. (*Look what he had to do*, she would say, *to free the slaves: all those dead Americans. You think that was fun?*) Johnny, Carol Harris, and a couple of old Army buddies were just about it for me as far as friends were concerned. Once in a while, they made me smile. Lincoln must have had a couple of friends, too. Carol and I are going to talk tonight. She texted to say she had some answers for me. I was looking forward to hearing her voice. She had not only fixed my brain but my soul as well.

# CHAPTER 11

"She can't live here., it's a decrepit barn," I said. "I can see snow drifts inside."

"That's the address I got," said Johnny.

Half of the barn's roof was gone, and the plank walls so dilapidated I could see right through them to a row of dead fruit trees, their feet in a foot of snow, their gnarled heads bowing to the winter cold.

I had almost made it home when Johnny called to tell me my nurse was Grace Carter, living at an address in Putnam Valley, a sprawling, rural township about twenty miles from my house. She left work early today, Johnny said. So I turned around. On the way, it started snowing again, a heavy mushy sleety kind of snow.

"Where are you, exactly?" Johnny asked.

"Across the street."

"I'm looking at Google Earth," said Johnny. "There's a small house about a half mile behind the barn."

"There must be a road."

"There is, about a quarter mile west."

"I'll check it out."

I was in old farm country, with the houses miles apart and lots of open space in between. I clicked Johnny off and pulled ahead, first waiting for a plow truck to pass me. The sleet that it was spitting up in its wake splattered hard against the windshield of my truck. There were two sets of tire tracks on the road he mentioned. Whether they were going in or out, I couldn't tell. I could see the house in the distance, small and squat, standing naked, smoke coming out of its chimney. Two cars were parked in front. One looked like a Hummer, the other, a regular car. I was halfway to the house when three people came out of the front door—two men in short jackets and woolen caps and a woman with short brown hair in boots, pants, and a red sweater. The woman's hands were tied behind her back. The men were shoving her toward the Hummer. About ten feet from it, one of the shoves propelled her stumbling forward. She lost her footing, hit her head against the car's rear fender, and fell to the ground on her side. One of the men bent to pick her up while the other was lifting the tailgate. If I had had a rifle with me, I would have shot both men, but I only had my Glock 26, so I sped up. About twenty yards away, I fishtailed so that my passenger side faced them. I dove out my side, went to the back corner of my truck and shot both men in the forehead. They had both drawn pistols but had no time to fire them before they were hit.

I searched their bodies and found nothing but their wallets, which I took. I left their weapons—both Sig

Sauers P220's—in the snow. I then untied Grace Carter (I assumed she was Grace Carter) and turned her over. She was out cold, a large nasty bruise on her forehead. There were reindeer on her sweater, which means nothing except this was the second red Christmas sweater I had come across in the last two days, and I wondered if some kind of sartorial theme was starting to develop in my life. There was another theme as well. Her sweater had risen at the waist, revealing a scar from her belly button extending diagonally up and ending at her rib cage.

## CHAPTER 12

"Where is she now?" Eva asked me.

"Sleeping. I gave her some Advil."

"You don't think she needs a doctor?"

"No."

"It's to the head, Popi."

"She woke up in my truck for a while. She'll be OK."

"Are you sure?"

"I know head injuries."

"What did she say?"

"Not much. She was out of it."

"Did you talk to Johnny?"

"Yes. He's looking into it."

"Does this have to do with the mosque guy?"

"Yes."

"Should I come up?"

"The snow is bad."

"I'll make it."

"Where's Hector?"

"He left this morning."

"I have to go," I said. "I hear her. Yes, come up."

In my bedroom, which is only ten steps away from where I was sitting in my kitchen, Grace was sitting up in bed with Moishe Dayan on her lap.

"He was scratching at the door," she said, nodding toward the door in my bedroom that opens onto a small back porch. "What's his name?" she asked.

"Moishe."

"Moishe?"

"A friend of my father's."

"He's got a bad eye."

I nodded. I had tried to get Moishe to come inside for five years. He would never cross the threshold. If I could have ever gotten a hold of him, I would have taken him to the vet. "Are you Grace Carter?" I asked.

"Yes."

"We have to talk."

# CHAPTER 13

After I talked to Grace Carter, I got calls from Joe Seritella and Johnny. I should tell you here that Johnny has invented an app that can scramble any cell phone conversation so that the only thing that any eavesdropper will hear is a song from a greatest opera aria play list. Neither party's number is identifiable or traceable. He downloaded it to my phone a few years ago and to Joe Seritella's when we had coffee in Queens. The app is called the Z App or Zap, named after me. It's not that we think anyone would be targeting us (although I sometimes think they might target me because they've probably gotten wind of some of the things I've done since I opened my own business and a—hopefully small—number of people are going to resent you no matter what you do, it's just human nature), it's just that being super cautious is always a good thing.

Later that night, I met Eva's friend Edison at Ska, a bar not far from Eva's place in the Bronx. Two big black guys at the door let me in with a nod toward the back. The place was empty except for two other big black guys playing pool in an alcove across from the bar. They stopped playing to look at me as I made my way to Edison's booth in the back corner. Eva, who was watching Grace Carter, had told me that Ska was an invitation-only bar, that being invited in means you will get out unharmed. No weapons, she said. They will take them and not give them back.

"What is your greatest fear?" Edison asked me when I was seated across from him.

"Dying alone," I said.

"Nothing else?"

"No. And yours?"

"Prison," he said.

"It's the same thing," I said.

A big smile appeared on the Jamaican's face. Like most black people, he had beautiful teeth.

"Why are you here?" he asked.

"I would like to hire you."

"To do what?"

"Put a GPS on a plane. And take a couple of pictures."

"A plane?"

"The things that fly."

"Where?"

"Out east on Long Island. There's an airport out there that's closed. This plane uses it at night."

"If it's closed, how can it land? It's not easy to land in the dark."

"Someone's helping the pilot, turning on the lights."

"How long will I have?"

"You'll do it yourself?"

"No, I will send my colleagues."

"Five minutes. The guy lands, then brings something over to someone waiting by a fence, then returns to the plane, turns it around, and takes off."

"Where on the plane?"

"On one of the wheel struts would be fine. It clamps on. You just need a flathead screwdriver."

"It's open terrain?"

"Yes."

"What if the pilot sees us?"

"Detain him and call me."

"So we might be kidnapping the pilot."

"Not if your guys are any good."

"Ten thousand."

"I can't pay you that. I can give you five. There's a lot of money that I believe I can get my hands on once I track the plane. If you will wait, I will pay you twenty thousand."

"Wait how long?"

"A week, maybe two."

"Get your hands on for sure?"

"Nothing's for sure."

"You will still owe me another five thousand."

"That I can't promise, but you will have my friendship. I can help you out in ways that other people can't."

"Eva tells me you are very skilled."

"I won't kill someone for a fee, but other than that."

"Other than that what?"

I looked around the room. The two big black guys who had let me in were at the bar, looking at me in the mirror. The other two were still playing pool.

"I could disable all five of you in under ninety seconds," I said.

"You have no weapon."

"Yes I do. Me."

"What is your relationship with Eva?"

I didn't answer, just looked at him.

"I don't mean personal," he said. He was smiling. Those teeth again. He didn't tag *mon* onto the end of every sentence the way a lot of Jamaicans do, but his accent was beautiful, pure Caribbean.

"Humint," I said.

"Humint?"

"Human intelligence," I replied. "She gets me information I could never get on my own. We're friends, too." I said this last thing so he'd get the message not to press me any further on the subject of Eva.

"I will be in touch," said Ska.

Which meant he got the message.

# CHAPTER 14

If you live in the Northeast, you know how short the days are here in the winter. Four-thirty and it's all over, dark as shit. I shudder to think of what it's like in Alaska. I drove in this darkness from Ska to Bronx River Avenue. Seritella had told me that Mohammed Asani sometimes hung out in a coffee shop, Al-Bustan, two blocks from his mosque. I parked a block away and trudged through the slush and snow. I had left my Glock in my truck when I went into Ska, but had it with me now in the front right pocket of my leather jacket. Inside, a veiled woman was working a coffee machine and men were sitting around tables smoking hookah and playing cards.

I ordered a coffee with no face, the Lebanese way, in Arabic. The veiled woman smiled at me with her eyes.

"You are Lebanese?" she asked.

"Yes," I said.

She poured the thick brew into a small cup. As she was handing it to me, I told her I was looking for Imam Mohammed Asani. Now she looked at me differently, her eyes, which were dark and beautiful, darting over my left shoulder.

"In the corner," she said.

Asani wore the traditional Muslim *al-lihyah*, the beard that covered the entire face except for the upper lip. His scar was clearly visible.

"*As-salamu alaykum*," I said to him. "May I sit?" His cell phone was on the table next to his coffee. I had my back to them, but I could tell that everyone in the small room, all men, except for the veiled woman behind the counter, were looking at me. I put my coffee down on his table, but remained standing.

"Who are you?"

"I need a kidney," I said.

Silence.

"Grace sent me."

"You have mistaken me for someone else."

"I saw you at the Pound Ridge Community Center on Wednesday with her."

"Again, you . . ."

I interrupted him, and said: "you slapped her across the face."

Something changed in Asani's eyes when I said this. Hopefully he was remembering me staring at him at the community center.

"Here are two friends of mine," said Asani. He was referring to two unbearded men, in their twenties, who had approached us from behind and were now standing on either side of me.

"They are going to escort you out."

"Grace told me you would help me," I said. "My wife is dying."

Asani nodded and the men each took hold of one of my arms. I flinched at first, but started breathing and was able to relax, or what passes for "relax" with me.

The two young guys walked me through a back room and out into a courtyard behind the building. Once there, I elbowed one in the throat and the other I threw head first into a brick wall. I was itching to kill them, but they were so unprofessional (they hadn't searched me, or drawn any weapons) I didn't think it was necessary. The one whose throat I had smashed was spazzing out on the ground, gasping for air. The other one was out cold, the top of his head oozing blood. I searched them, taking their wallets and cell phones. The one with the bleeding head had two wallets. One was his, the other was Joe Seritella's. He also had two cell phones. I assumed one was Joe's. There was an alley that led back to Bronx River Avenue. I put this guy over my shoulder and carried him to my car. No one saw me. If they had, they would not have noticed. As I've said before, not noticing is a skill passed on from generation to generation in the ghetto. Or possibly it's acquired. The old nature versus nurture thing. It doesn't really matter, because it was freezing cold and no one was out on the street. Of course, gang bangers notice. They are always looking for prey. Citizens do not notice. Another dumb digression. Sorry.

I was only driving a few minutes when Johnny called. He told me that Joe Seritella's body had been found behind a warehouse in Mount Vernon. I pulled over and shot the passed-out guy in the back of my truck in the stomach, then drove to Asani's so-called Islamic Center and left him to bleed out at the front door.

# CHAPTER 15

I hate to say it, but I doubt there are many people in Co-op City who know who Theodore Dreiser is/was. I read a lot as a kid, so I do, but since my head injury I can't concentrate the way I used to, so the only thing I read now is poetry. I also write poetry, which sounds ridiculous, but I do. It calms me. Sometimes, lying in bed at night, my thoughts will get away from me. This is a euphemism. They race around the inside of my head like Tazmanian devils. (This may not be a good metaphor as I don't know much about Tazmanian devils, but the name itself does suggest a lot of running around like crazy, so one way or another I think it works). On really bad nights I'll compose a poem as a diversion. Sometimes it works, only to have the devils show up in a dream, which I accept as an overall positive. I wrote a poem last week called My Deals With Devils And Other Survival Strategies. No one has ever read any of them, and neither will you. Don't worry, you're not missing anything. The trade-off (to my head injury) is, I now have mental and physical instincts and reflexes that are about fifty times what they used to be, and they were pretty fast pre-plate-in-the-head. For example, the elbow I threw to the throat of the guy back at the courtyard would not have been caught on camera had it been filmed at regular speed. You would have seen us walking, then you would have seen him on the ground. I have also pretty much lost all fear. I meant it when I told Eva's friend Edison that I was afraid of dying alone, but I left out the real thing I fear, which is dying alone during or after a seizure. Other than that, I have no fear of anything. The psycho-biological dynamic that ramps up fear in the normal person has been replaced in me by some kind of super adrenalin that powers out whenever I sense danger or need to act quickly. You might think this is bullshit, but the two guys I killed at Grace Carter's house and the two I knocked around in the rear of Al-Bustan would probably disagree. There have been others, but those are other stories for other days.

Anyway, Joe Seritella lived in a townhouse on Dreiser Loop in Co-op City in the Bronx. I met Johnny outside. Inside it was awkward. Don't forget, I had only met Seritella once and talked to him on the phone a couple of times, which really doesn't count. The same goes for Johnny. Seritella's wife and thirty-year-old autistic son sat with us in the living room, while an old Italian lady sat sobbing at the kitchen table. The son stared at me like we were kindred spirits, which didn't surprise me. Johnny told the wife that we were from the NYPD's Widow's And Orphan's Fund, and left her an envelope with cash in it.

Back on the street, I asked him how much was in the envelope. A thousand, he said. It was all he could scrape together. I made a mental note to bring more as soon as I could.

# CHAPTER 16

The owner of Levendusky Airfield had died a year ago, and his two sons, one in California and one in Florida, were fighting over who would inherit it, along with the cash old man Levendusky had socked away over sixty years of frugality imprinted on his psyche as a kid growing up in the Great Depression. While they were fighting in court, the airport was closed. A pseudo-security guard, one Pete Flynn, was hired to watch the place at night, but he wasn't paid much (the sons were cheap, and Pete was a drinker and pretty much homeless) and it had been easy for Joe Seritella to befriend him. Over a bottle of scotch, Pete had told Joe the story of the airport's origins in the fifties, of the court battle, and of the fact that about six months ago, a guy had appeared one night and offered him a hundred bucks a pop to turn the runway lights on a couple of times a month and of course to look the other way should a plane land and promptly take off. The guy even gave Pete a cell phone, on which he would call him about two hours ahead of an arrival. Pete didn't know where the plane was coming from, but guessed no more than two flight hours away, since it couldn't refuel as there was no longer any fuel trucks at Levendusky. Joe gave Pete a hundred dollars and told him to call him on his cell phone the next time this plane was going to land. When Joe told me all this (on the same day he was killed by Asani's assholes) I asked him how he knew Flynn could be trusted. He didn't, he said, but he was going back with Flynn's rap sheet. He jumped bail fifteen years ago on a burglary charge, which meant he was going straight to jail if he fucked Joe. As you know, Joe never got back there, so I took a ride out the next day, first making stops at Seritella's apartment to drop off another envelope with cash in it, and then at Ska to give Edison his 5K retainer.

At this point, you're probably thinking, where did this Z-Man guy with the plate in his head get all this money? I get my VA disability check of course, but I also get paid for what I do. On top of that, if I recover money for a client, or if money turns up during the job, I take a cut. The first time this happened was actually on my first case, which was for Carol Harris. We each netted over a hundred thousand when it turned out her abusive husband had ten or twelve secret bank accounts in the Los Angeles area, which Carol received after he died unexpectedly. Maybe that will be my next story, which I think would be interesting, but you never know. My diversions may be exasperating to people, a turnoff. I try to get a leash on them but it's not easy. They are strong like bulls. Anyway, that's how I've come to have a few dollars, most of which I keep in cash in my house. My mother didn't believe in banks and neither do I. When my parents bought their first house on Long Island, my mother showed up at the closing with thirty-two thousand in cash in a pillow case, money she had saved while my dad was fighting with the Sayeret Matkal, Israel's Delta Force, in Lebanon and other Middle East venues. Most of what I know about aggressive soldiering I learned from my dad. Google Sayeret Matkal and you'll see exactly what he did for the first ten years of his career. I also live cheaply. My most expensive things are my two cars and my weapons. Everything else is pretty much your basic stuff, which doesn't in any way need to be fancy.

# CHAPTER 17

At Levendusky Field, I gave Flynn another hundred and asked him to show me around. He told me that after the old man died, the son in Florida had wanted to keep the airport going and had begun to renovate one of the hangars when the other brother got a court order to stop him. I showed him my fake F.B.I. ID and told him that the guys who were using the airport at night were Muslim terrorists under investigation by the Bureau. I believed him when he told me he'd never met the pilot. The description he had given to Joe Seritella of the guy who gave him the cell phone fitted about a million people—white with a beard—was worthless, so I didn't pursue it. I got right to the point: unless he sobered up and cooperated he would go to jail for life when the terrorists were arrested. I told him there was a 5K reward for information leading to their arrest. I mentioned his rap sheet and bail-jumping acrobatics.

Pete is a guy who's lived on the street a long time, and like most (if not all) homeless people is obviously deranged. But not stupid. I gave him Edison's number and told him all he had to do to earn the 5K reward was to call the number and say when the next plane would be arriving. When I told him that a couple of big black guys might be paying him a visit, he didn't bat an eye.

Before I left, I transferred all of the data from the cell phone that Pete had been given to a small extraction device, called a UFED. In my truck, I downloaded the data to a laptop I keep plugged in at all times, and sent it to Johnny via Dropbox. I called him to confirm that he had received the data intact, and asked him to meet me at my house.

# CHAPTER 18

Eva and Johnny were playing chess on the rug in front of the fire when I got home. Grace was sitting on the couch. Moishe Dayan was sleeping on her lap with his head sticking out from under one of my mother's multi-colored Afghans. He opened his good eye for a second to look at me then went back to sleep. I was pouring myself whiskey over ice when my cell phone rang.

"Plane landing in two hours," said Edison. "My colleagues are halfway there."

I had called him to tell him to look for a call from a certain number. I looked at my watch.

"There's a plane landing at one a.m.," I said to my houseguests.

"It's a kidney," said Grace.

"Maybe it's the guy I left at the mosque," I said. "He wasn't dead."

"What guy?" Johnny asked.

"I have to pick up someone at LaGuardia," I said. "Can you come with me?"

"Sure," Johnny answered. *"What guy?"*

"I'll tell you in the car."

"I have some information for you, too," said Johnny.

"I have to leave in the morning," said Eva.

I nodded and turned to Grace. "How are you?" I asked.

"Better."

I nodded. She had some color back. I wasn't close enough to smell her, but I wish I was. I noticed that Moishe's ears picked up when he heard her voice. "You have to stay here," I said.

"I know."

"Asani is looking for you right now."

"I know."

"The police, too."

She nodded.

"I'll be back in a couple of hours."

Out of the corner of my eye I saw Eva staring at me. Was she jealous? She toys with me, uses me for sex, and now she's jealous? Fuck.

# CHAPTER 19

I'm going to go backward for a second. I didn't want to, it's personal, but it's something important you should know about the time I spent with Grace the day I killed the two guys at her house, the two hours we spent together before Eva arrived. I had tried talking to her in the bedroom, but got only to telling her my name when she said she wanted to take a shower. This decision (to fill in these two hours) is coming from my gut, as I don't know anything about telling stories or writing them down. When the idea of doing this (writing this story) first occurred to me, I went online and Googled *how to write a story*. I was shocked at how much there was written on the subject. Some of it made sense, but most of it gave me a headache. I erased it all with a couple of stiff whiskeys and the next day sat down at my laptop and began firing away. I decided I would be the first man, writing the first story and to let the chips fall where they may.

I told Grace before she went in the bathroom that there was a robe on a hook behind the door that she could use. Moishe scratched at the bathroom door until she opened it six inches to let him in. I got a quick glimpse of her, naked and wet. While she was in there, I laid out one of my flannel shirts, a sweater, and a pair of old sweat pants. Also thick woolen socks. Gray Wigwams. Her red sweater had bloodstains on it. When she let Moishe in, I was pulling the flannel shirt out of a drawer, so I was nearby and reflexively looked. There was eye contact. She actually half smiled before she closed the door. I still think of that half smile to this day. I smelled steam and shampoo before she closed the door, and something else, something I came to recognize and call *Grace*. It's not a big deal, but as I've said, my head injury heightened a lot of things for me. You don't want to be punched in the face by me, because I actually think I can take your head off. I also smell and see and hear things way different than the normal person. Something was coming out of Grace's body that made me dizzy.

She came out of the bathroom in the robe, saw the things I had laid out, and took them back into the bathroom. I had made a fire and put a bottle of whiskey and two glasses on the coffee table. We sat on the couch. I poured drinks. I had no idea where to begin so I said nothing.

"Who are you?" Grace asked.

"I told you, Zev Evans. My friends call me Z."

"Z."

"Z, Z-man, Zevon," I said. I was nervous.

"I like Zev. Or Zevvie."

"No one's ever called me that."

"Your shower felt good."

I nodded. "I saw your scar," I said. "Not in the bathroom just now. At your house when you were out cold. Your sweater had hiked up. Sorry about that." I blurted this out. I wanted her to know as soon as possible that I wasn't a pervert who looked at women's bodies when they were unconscious. And that I was interested in her scar.

"What were you doing at my house?" she asked. I was surprised she ignored the scar issue, but still relieved to have gotten it on the table.

"I wanted to talk to you," I said.

"Why?"

"I saw Asani slap you at the recital."

"The recital? I'm confused. You know Asani?"

"I just met him."

"I'm dying, Mr. Z," she said, "so please just tell me what's going on."

"Dying?"

"I had a kidney transplant two years ago, but it's failing."

She was two feet away from me across the couch. The smell she was oozing from the soap and hot water was fading, but I could still breathe in Grace from where I sat. I told her who I was and what I did. I told her everything I had done since I saw Asani slap her. I told her that I had figured out what Asani was up to. When I was done, I poured myself another drink. Her glass was empty so I poured her one, too.

"Where do you fit in?" I asked.

"Asani was supposed to give me a kidney."

"You can have two transplants?"

She nodded. "Yes, it's been done."

"What about the regular way?"

"I went to the bottom of the list, plus . . . already getting one . . . no one thinks I'm a good candidate. I have six months."

"To live?"

"In six months, I'll need dialysis five days a week. Six months after that, I'll be dead."

There was nothing to say to this. I took a sip of my drink, and put it down. "What did you do for Asani?" I asked.

"I assisted in the surgeries, with Rashida. Asani kept putting me off, kept harvesting kidneys and selling them."

"From whom?"

"Immigrants, Mexican mostly. Guatemalan. Illegals."

"From the Bronx?"

"From all over. He pays recruiters a thousand dollars a kidney. He pays the donors five thousand."

"What does he sell them for?"

"I don't know."

"Do you know who he sells them to?"

"No."

"Rashida Nahra. What's her deal?"

"I don't know."

"Does he have something on her?"

"She lives in fear of him, I don't know why."

"Did she hook you up with him?"

"Yes, we worked together. She knew my situation. A second O.R. nurse was needed. It's complicated surgery."

"Dr. Samad does the surgeries?"

"Yes."

"Where?"

"At the Islamic Center. He lives there."

"I take it those were Asani's guys at your house."

"Yes."

"What did you do?"

"I told him I was going to stop, that I was getting too weak."

"He didn't believe you."

"No."

"*Are* you getting weak?"

"I have to have dialysis twice a week. I'm due Thursday."

"You were doing it at Northern Westchester?"

"Yes, but . . ."

"No, you can't go back there."

"No, but they'll wonder."

"Let them. Anybody else?"

"I have a sister and brother-in-law in Connecticut."

"You can't call them. Maybe later."

She nodded. She understood the hole she was in.

"Are you married?" I asked.

"Divorced."

"Are you in touch?"

"No. He's in California."

"Kids?"

"No."

"I'll make some arrangements."

"Arrangements?"

"For your dialysis. I have a doctor friend. She'll figure out what to do."

"What about those two guys?" Grace asked.

"I have another friend at the NYPD. He's on top of it."

"I wish I had friends like you."

"You do now," I said.

She must have seen the way I was looking at her because she said, "I've lost a lot of weight. I'm . . ."

"You're what?"

"I'm nothing to look at." She was crying.

The thing is, she *was* something to look at, even sick. Big eyes, beautiful full lips. Her gauntness made my heart ache.

This is where I stop. I couldn't describe or "narrate" what happened next anyway. Even if I could, I wouldn't. Like I said, it's personal. Once I started really breathing in Grace, I was lost to myself and the world and didn't want to return.

# CHAPTER 20

"So what guy did you drop off at the mosque who wasn't dead?" Johnny asked.

When we visited Joe Seritella's widow, I didn't tell Johnny about my encounter with Asani's two friends. I wasn't sure if he needed to know. He knew about the two guys at Grace's house in Putnam Valley. I had to tell him about them in case someone had seen me (there was that snowplow driver, for instance) and I needed his help. Johnny and Carol Harris and Eva are my only real friends, and I have a complicated way of building walls around them when it comes to my activities. The less they knew, the less they could get in trouble. But now Johnny needed to know about the two guys at al-Bustan, so I told him.

We were on the Merritt Parkway, which had been cleared, but still had snow swirling on and over it. I was driving my Jeep.

"Is the other one dead?" Johnny asked.

"No."

"That's three in two days, Z."

I nodded. "What's going on in Putnam Valley?" I asked.

"Nothing. The bodies haven't been discovered. Do you want me to clean that up?"

"No, it's too risky."

"I can do it."

"No, it can't be tied to me, unless someone saw me."

"When they find the bodies, they'll start talking to people."

"I'm thinking Asani might have cleaned it up when they didn't come back."

"Let's hope so. What about the gun you used?"

"Gone."

"Really?"

"I know how to dispose of a weapon, John."

Johnny let this go. He knew I didn't like to throw away guns and was needling me. "I assume you wanted to talk to the guy you shot in the stomach," he said.

"Yes. He had Joe's wallet and cell phone."

"I see. You got pissed."

"Yes, I lost it when you called to tell me Joe's body had been found."

"What's the back seat of your truck look like?"

"Some blood. A lot."

"Where is it?"

"Behind the cottage, on the dirt road I use sometimes."

"I'll send the boys up tomorrow." He was referring to his twin sons, who were now twenty and skilled in a lot of things that most people, let alone kids, are ever exposed to, most of it learned from me. They were my godsons, which puts me in line to be their father if anything ever happened to Johnny. It's a Sicilian thing, which everybody knows about from the movies, but nevertheless true.

"They can pick up your car while they're there," I said.

"Good idea."

We drove along, pretty much alone on the road, the snow piled on the shoulders.

"That Grace is sick," Johnny said after a while.

"I know."

"A wounded bird."

"I know."

"Who are we picking up?"

"Carol Harris."

"Your doctor friend."

"Yes."

"Talk to me."

I told him about Grace, about Edison and my plan.

"What do you want me to do?"

"Carol needs to make some arrangements. She needs to get upstate to a clinic run by an old Army friend of hers, a doctor named Frank Haines. Can you help her out?"

"Of course."

"What about Asani's money?" I asked.

"It's in the Caymans and Switzerland."

"How much?"

"A million in the Caymans. A million in Switzerland."

"Can you get in?"

"No. It's a voice authentication system, both banks."

"So we'll need him alive?"

"Either that, or, if I can get him on tape, I can replicate his voice."

"Really?"

"Yes. The password I can hack, but it'll have to be entered in his voice."

"Or I can put a gun to his head."

"You're the boss."

"That might be fun."

"I only need him talking for ten minutes, Z."

"And then what?"

"I have software that can recreate his voice in a few minutes."

"Really?"

"I type in what has to be said and it morphs into his voice."

"Guaranteed?"

"No. But the gun might not work either."

I thought about this. If I had to, I would put the gun to Asani's dick, just the tip. That would work. I needed his money. It was a big part of my plan.

"Did you look at Pete Flynn's phone?" I said.

"Yes, it's a throwaway. The same for the phones they call him on."

"Plural."

"Plural."

"A dead end."

"Yes."

"It won't matter," I said, "if Edison's guys do what they're being paid for."

We drove some more, then Johnny said, "you don't need women trouble. You couldn't handle it."

"Who *could*?" I said.

"Not you."

"You're talking about Eva?"

"She had daggers in her eyes."

"I thought so. I wasn't sure."

"I'll leave it at that."

"Actually," said Johnny after a short while, "I can't leave it."

"My women problem?"

"Yes."

I kept quiet, hoping for some kind of diversion, but nothing materialized.

"She's Latina," said Johnny. "She'll take a knife to you."

"She's married," I said. "She won't leave her husband."

"Have you asked her to?"

"No."

Johnny kept still, but I knew what he was thinking.

"She's hot, then she's cold," I said. "It's not love, John."

"You better be honest with her," said Johnny. "It's the best of a lot of bad options."

"You mean she might not try to kill me if I'm honest."

"Honest and lucky."

# CHAPTER 21

Picking up people at LaGuardia is not easy. You have to time it perfectly, otherwise the Port Authority cops will aggressively wave you on. We made a pass, didn't see Carol, and moved on. I had told her that if I wasn't there when she came outside, to call me on my cell, that I would be waiting nearby in a parking area that limo drivers used. While we were waiting, Edison called. The GPS was in place. He also texted a picture of the plane's fuselage, showing its registration number. Johnny opened his laptop and immediately began tracking the plane. The software Johnny used was like the kind used on international commercial flights. We watched an airplane icon move like Pac-Man on Johnny's screen on a line due north toward Albany. He opened a second window and in a few minutes found that the plane, a Cirrus SR20, belonged to one Adnan Berovic of Charlton, New York.

"Where's Charlton?" I asked.

"Outside Albany."

"Who is he?"

*Click, click, click.* "A retired professor at SUNY Buffalo," said Johnny.

"What kind?"

"Medicine. Nephrology."

After a few more clicks, Johnny showed me Berovic's picture. Black hair, black eyes. He looked like a pirate, not a professor.

"Where does he live?"

More clicks. "It looks like a farm," said Johnny, "two hundred acres."

"That's probably where the plane's heading." We were watching Pac-Man advance north.

"Can you talk to your friends in the State Police?" I asked.

"No problem. What do you want?"

"I want them to put a net over the professor, but not to drop it until we give the word. I want the plane disabled, too."

"I'll call now."

As Johnny was on his phone, mine rang. It was Carol.

# CHAPTER 22

"Popi, shall I divorce Hector?"

Shall I divorce Hector? This was the first time I had ever heard Eva use the word *shall*. It was probably the first time anyone from the Tremont section of the Bronx had ever used it. When I got back to the cottage, Grace was asleep in my bed and Eva on the couch. There was a pink flower in a Silver Patron bottle on the coffee table. The fire was dying. I added a couple of logs and laid out my sleeping bag between the coffee table and the fireplace. As I was doing this, Eva woke up. Before she asked her question with the word shall in it, we had the following conversation:

"How is she?" I asked, referring to Grace, nodding toward my closed bedroom door.

"Not well."

"I'm going to help her."

"How?"

"She has to go upstate to a private clinic."

"When?"

"Tomorrow."

"Will she get dialysis there?"

"Yes. Did she tell you her story?"

"Yes. Popi, I'm sorry."

"For what?"

"I hated you."

"We . . ."

"Don't tell me."

Eva was sitting up now on the couch, wearing one of my flannel shirts. With, I could tell, no bra. I could be on my deathbed and I would notice something like this.

"Don't tell you what?" I said.

"About you and Grace."

"I . . ."

"And don't lie either," she said.

I said nothing.

"I know anyway," she said.

More silence from me. You can't fuck up if you say nothing. Most of the time, that is.

"Can I help?" Eva said.

"You can drive her up there and stay with her."

"When?"

"Tomorrow."

"Of course. What are you going to do?"

I ignored this. "I want you to bring Jose's boy upstate as well," I said. "Can you do that?"

"Jose will do what I say."

"Good."

"Do you want Jose's money?"

"No."

"OK. Then what?"

"Then wait for me to call."

"Sit next to me," she said. I was sitting on my sleeping bag. I got up and sat next to her. That's when she asked her question, the one with the word shall in it, stopping me in my tracks.

"Yes," I said, surprising myself.

"We're not really husband and wife anyway," she said. "I only married him to get my citizenship."

"He's American?"

"He was born here."

"He acted like he had certain rights," I said. "The few times I met him."

"You are jealous. Good."

I shook my head. I never thought I could afford to be jealous. I'm not a handsome guy with women falling all over me. But she was right, I was.

Eva took my hand and put it on her chest.

# CHAPTER 23

Carol Harris called late the next day to tell me that Grace, Moishe Dayan, and Miguel were settled in at Dr. Haines' clinic. Jose was in a Holiday Inn in Schenectady. Eva had offered to pick up Donato the dog and bring him to her place. Johnny's boys had done the chauffeuring. I called them to thank them and to ask them to stand by because I might have another favor to ask. I could see the smiles on their faces. They were afraid of nothing. I decided I had to act. I assumed Asani was spooked. The two assholes he had sent to abduct Grace had not returned. A third had had his larynx crushed and a fourth turned up gut-shot at his mosque. (He must have had an open order for a kidney and decided to take advantage of his luck (good and bad) at finding a free one at his front door). But now he had to be thinking of running.

He lived in a modest little house on a street of modest little houses with no front yards and only narrow alleys separating them. Chain- link fences in front and barred first floor windows were the rule. This was Mount Vernon, the Bronx light. Joe Seritella had described the house and neighborhood, and Johnny had had some satellite pictures taken and gotten the building plans from 1967, so I knew the layout inside and out. Seritella had spotted two bodyguards living with Mohammed, and a pit bull in the fenced-in backyard. I did not doubt that the two bodyguards had killed Joe.

The pit bull went crazy when I approached through the alley from the street behind. I let him howl for a minute or two, then put a tranquilizer dart into his flank. He was so worked up I thought I might have to hit him with another one, but his howls finally turned to whimpers and he went to sleep on his side. I actually had to step over him after dropping down from the fence. I watched from the shadows as the bodyguards came out the back door, weapons drawn. I had brought night vision goggles but didn't need them, the moonlight was so bright. I shot both of them in the forehead with my silenced M9 from about fifty feet away. You have probably noticed by now that I am a forehead-shooter. The reason for this is many bad guys are wearing bulletproof vests nowadays. They also carry small canons for weapons, which I don't want them to use. I can hit you at fifty feet in the middle of the forehead as long as there's enough light for me to see and as long as you're standing relatively still, which these two were. They should have gone in different directions when they came out the door and crouched low, but they didn't. I would have killed them both whatever they did, but they made it much easier for me. Stupid. Arrogant. Anyway, there's another digression for you. Sorry.

In his second floor bedroom, I had to wake Asani up. I realized why when I saw the vial of Ambien on his night table. I took this with me as you never know when pharmaceuticals might be needed in various situations. I took Asani with me too, of course.

# CHAPTER 24

"Mohammed," I said, "we meet again. Do you remember me now? From the recital?"

Asani was not happy, but he still had some spunk left. I could see it in his eyes. He was used to getting his way, and had not yet realized that in this case he wouldn't.

"At the Pound Ridge Community Center?" I said.

He spit at me then, hitting me in the chest. He was duct-taped to a chair, arms and legs. I would have duct-taped his mouth shut, but I needed him to talk so that Johnny, who was standing next to me with a digital voice recorder in his shirt pocket, could record his voice.

I had a washcloth and a pitcher of water on a table nearby. I wiped Asani's spit from my shirt with the washcloth, then said, "your bodyguards are dead."

Silence. The hot-eyed type.

"Your dog is OK."

More of the same.

"I could waterboard you," I said. "It's easy."

No answer.

"Rashida and Dr. Samad are next door, in your little clinic."

No answer. Hate in his eyes.

"Rashida says you promised to bring her two girls over from Jordan."

Nothing.

"Did you?"

Nothing.

"Now she doesn't know where they are. She thinks you're holding them someplace. She hates your guts, Mohammed."

Nothing.

"Dr. Samad is tired of this gig, too," I said. "He's ready to pack it in. He says you haven't paid him what you said you would."

"You are not an F.B.I. agent," said Asani.

"No," I said, "I'm not."

"You have kidnapped me."

"How did you figure that out?" I said. "You must be really smart."

It had been easy for Johnny to disable the mosque's wireless alarm. It relied on a radio frequency signal that

Johnny jammed from his car behind the building. We had to break the plate glass window with a sledgehammer to get in. We duct-taped it first to dull the noise, but the thuds were loud enough to wake up Samad. In his boxer shorts, he looked pretty shocked to see us, which made it easy for us to quickly subdue him. He wasn't a combatant anyway, just an asshole who'd rather make money the easy way taking out people's kidneys, than the hard way, by working ten hours a day, the way most doctors do. A few minutes later I called Johnny's boys and told them it was safe to join us with Rashida.

Asani was glaring at me. He didn't like my sarcastic tone, I could tell.

"You took your first kidney from your wife, didn't you Mohammed? You drugged her and she woke up with a kidney missing and an eight-inch scar. She must have been really bummed out, so she killed herself. Or maybe she was going to turn you in and you killed her, crushed up that Ambien and put it in her coffee. We know about your first business, selling marriage visas. But there's so much more money in kidneys, right Mohammed?"

Hatred.

"We've picked up Professor Berovic," I went on. "I don't want to say kidnapped as once we put a gun in his mouth he came along willingly. He can't stop talking, the poor guy, some kind of disorder. Asperger's, maybe. He mentions your name a lot. Every sentence. He says you're the ringleader, the one making all the money. We're not sure if we believe him. Can you help us out?"

Nothing.

"He lives up near Albany," I said. "He owns a plane and has a private airstrip on his property. I'll show you

a video of the professor spilling his guts if you want."
(I did not have a video. And I was making it up about
Berovic spilling his guts and turning on Asani. The State
Police were waiting to pick up Berovic, who had no idea
that a house was about to fall on him).

"He's lying," said Asani.

"He said you'd say that."

I looked at Johnny, who had moved off to the side
after some of Mohammed's spit spray landed on his
arm. He shook his head.

"Here's the thing, Mohammed," I said, "Berovic says
you're financing terrorist cells with your kidney profits.
He says you backed those two in San Bernardino. You
know what that means . . ."

"He's lying."

"He said *you'd* be doing the lying, that we shouldn't
believe a thing you say."

"Do you want money?" Mohammed asked.

"Yes."

"Berovic is sometimes paid in cash. He keeps it buried on his farm. You'll never find it. I can take you there."

"How much?"

"Five hundred, six hundred thousand."

"That's all?"

"The rest is in Swiss accounts."

"Do you have access to them?"

"No, of course not." The fire had gone out of the
imam's eyes. He was now a businessman, trying to close
a deal.

"How do you know about the buried cash?" I asked.

"I followed him one day in the beginning."

"Where?"

"I will take you."

I looked at Johnny, who nodded, a smile on his face. I took a syringe that I had filled with Demerol out of my pharmaceutical kit, and held it up for Mohammed to see.

"It's just Demerol," I said, "don't worry, but if I inject it too fast, you could die, so don't make any sudden movements."

A quizzical look.

"When you wake up," I continued, "you'll either be in prison or on a plane back to Tunisia," I said, "you choose."

"I saw him go toward a rock wall in the woods behind the barn," Mohammed said. "He was lifting rocks. That's all. I couldn't get too close."

"Thank you, Mohammed," I said, "have a nice flight."

I hovered the needle over his neck, then inserted the tip and slowly pushed the plunger. "By the way," I said, when I was done, "where you're going you won't be needing your kidneys."

# CHAPTER 25

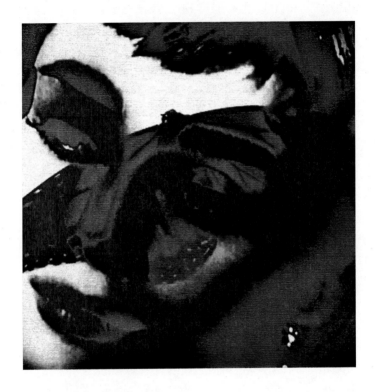

Grace's heart stopped on the operating table. They revived her, but she died a week later. She's being buried tomorrow in Farmington. I brought her sister up to Schenectady and filled her in on the way. I picked up Moishe Dayan while I was there. At home, I bought Moishe a bunch of cat toys, but he ignores them and just mopes and sleeps. He's not even interested in going outside. Miguel is recuperating at Dr. Haines' clinic. Jose is still at the Holiday Inn. Johnny accessed Asani's accounts, and we spread the money around, to Jose and Miguel, to Joe Seritella's widow, to Eva, to Edison, to Pete Flynn, to Grace's sister, to Johnny's boys (in trust till they turned thirty-five), to the Pound Ridge Community Center, to the NYC PBA Widows and Childrens' Fund, to the National Kidney Foundation, to Carol Harris, to Dr. Haines' clinic. We didn't give any to Samad or Rashida, but we let them go after they extracted Asani's kidneys. They understood completely when we said that we would have eyes on them for a long time. I hear from Johnny that his bureau is talking to them about working under cover. What was left of Asani's money, about 200K, Johnny and I split.

Eva was in Nevada getting a divorce, so I had Donato with me too. I was lonely. Carol Harris had flown back to California. It would have been nice to have her around, but she had to get back to her husband and two kids. When I dropped her off at the airport, she reminded me of what I said when I came out of my coma in Germany. *There was a beautiful breeze along the river.* I wasn't looking forward to going to Grace Carter's funeral, believe me. If I picked up the flannel shirt I gave her to wear, I could smell her. If Moishe, who had not left her side in Schenectady, sat with me, I could breathe her in. Even Donato, who slept all day with Moishe, smelled of her. I was thinking of her funeral, and of breathing her in, and of the breeze along the river that night in Iraq, and then I was with Grace, stroking the butterfly tattoo at the top of her right breast. Then I was kissing her, but it wasn't Grace; it was Donato licking me. I was on the floor in the kitchen on my back, sunlight from a skylight on my face. Moishe was on my stomach, looking at me. There was a funny taste in my mouth. I got up and

Moishe jumped up to the refrigerator and watched me as I made coffee. Donato was following me around.

"What happened?" I said to him, "did I have a seizure?"

He barked, which usually meant he wanted to go out. I went over to the front door and opened it for him, but he stayed put. Moishe jumped down to the kitchen table. This was the most he had moved in the last five days. I kept the door open in case he wanted to go out, but he stayed put too.

I made a fire and brought my coffee over to it. Tomorrow was a Tuesday. There was a recital at the Pound Ridge Community Center every Tuesday evening. After Grace's funeral I would stop by. I tried, but I hadn't saved her. I would listen to whatever music was being played and thank her for saving me.

# About the Author

James LePore is an attorney who has practiced law for more than two decades. He is also an accomplished photographer. He lives in Venice, FL with his wife, artist Karen Chandler. He is the author of five solo novels, *A World I Never Made, Blood of My Brother, Sons and Princes, Gods and Fathers,* and *The Fifth Man,* as well as a collection of short stories, *Anyone Can Die* and the collection of flash fiction, *Blood, Light & Time*. He is also the author, with Carlos Davis, of the Mythmakers Trilogy, *No Dawn for Men, God's Formula* and *The Bone Keepers*. You can visit him at his website, www.JamesLeporeFiction.com.